Sea of Echoes

ILLUSTRATED BY RUTHIE BRIGGS-GREENBERG
WRITTEN BY J. MAC REED

TAYLOR TRADE PUBLISHING
LANHAM • BOULDER • NEW YORK • LONDON

Finn spies old ocean's strangest of features:
Floating islands with two-legged creatures.

Published by
TAYLOR TRADE PUBLISHING
An imprint of The Rowman & Littlefield Publishing Group, Inc.
4501 Forbes Boulevard, Suite 200, Lanham, Maryland 20706
www.rowman.com

Unit A, Whitacre Mews, 26-34 Stannary Street,
London SE11 4AB, United Kingdom

Distributed by NATIONAL BOOK NETWORK

Illustrations copyright © 2016 by Ruthie Briggs-Greenberg
Text copyright © 2016 by J. Mac Reed

Original idea and layout by Ruthie Briggs-Greenberg;
edited by Randy Greenberg.

Teachers! A classroom curriculum is available from Rowman & Littlefield for use with *Sea of Echoes*. It includes fun and engaging discussion questions and exercises that conform to common core requirements. Please contact textbooks@rowman.com for details!

British Library Cataloguing in Publication Information Available

Library of Congress Cataloging-in-Publication Data Available

♾ The paper used in this publication meets the minimum requirements of American National Standard for Information Sciences—Permanence of Paper for Printed Library Materials, ANSI/NISO Z39.48-1992.

Printed in the United States of America

My dad, Art Briggs, in the Arctic, 1969

For Sophia and Arthur, from Mommy

Dedicated to the whales and the people who
love them -Ruthie

For Aryss and Emma -Jeff

This book manifested with support from my kids; My husband/editor/manager,
Randy; Those who helped this book along the path to print; Ornah; Taylor Trade
Publishing; My parents, family and friends; Professors and Boots at AAU; and Jeff,
who took a leap of faith in the story and us as a team! —Ruthie

1

Finn knew the time was approaching when he would have to leave the company of his mother.

But he knew that even after that, he would hear her calling to him. Prudence, Finn's mother, would never, ever be far from him or he from her. The call of the **fin whales** did not have the complexity of his cousins the humpbacks, yet in its rhythm and intonation and power, it conveyed its own melody and harmony into the symphony of the sea.

Finn and his mother had traveled together through many thousands of miles across the oceans of the world, sometimes just the two of them, sometimes in the company of other **whales**, but never had his mother and he been far apart.

Except for the blue whales—who were only slightly larger than their darker, streamlined cousins—the fin whales were the largest living beings in the ocean, and Finn knew that he would have little to fear from the other creatures that shared its briny waters. But he loved to watch them: these friends and neighbors of the sea, each creature of its kind living its life, the smallest among the greatest.

There were the swarms of jellyfish that pulsed through the water and always mystified Finn: they seemed nothing more to him than a slime-covered bag that swam indolently by him as he **logged** with the other whales, and they seemed to have no more interest in breaching or **spyhopping** than would a bed of kelp.

Of all the sights that will thrill you the most,
None is like spotting a whale on the coast.

To help her baby breathe, she gives a shove.
How Finn is blessed to have a mother's love.

There were the **cormorants**, the creatures who dived into Finn's watery world as fast and in as great a number as the drops of rain that fell over the ocean when the sky grew dark. One moment he would be swimming among the schools of herring as innumerable as his much-relished **krill**, and then suddenly he would be bombarded by these winged creatures which would snatch up the fish and then return quickly to the surface. Finn would rise and follow to watch them as they ascended beyond the expanse of the ocean and high into the sky, and he never understood why he could not go where they could go, no matter how hard he might hurl his body upward in an attempt to breach the ocean's surface, into the firmament above.

And when the herring came, so too came his cousins the dolphins, their bodies twisting and turning as they herded the fish into whirlwinds of revolving, silvery morsels. The dolphins seemed to have as much fun playing with their food as they did eating it.

For all the beauty of the sea, Finn had learned that there could be danger there too, even for one so large as himself—and not from his fellow sea-dwellers.

Finn was feeding and growing and playing and traveling, traveling to where the water was colder and colder, and great floes of ice passed them by. Though it was getting colder by the day the further they traveled, it mattered not to him, as his coat of **blubber** grew ever thicker, and plentiful were the blooms of krill to make it so.

He knew the time would soon come when he and his mother must part, for she had now raised him from a defenseless baby to an adolescent **bull calf**, though to him he was more bullish and to his mother he was still not far from a calf.

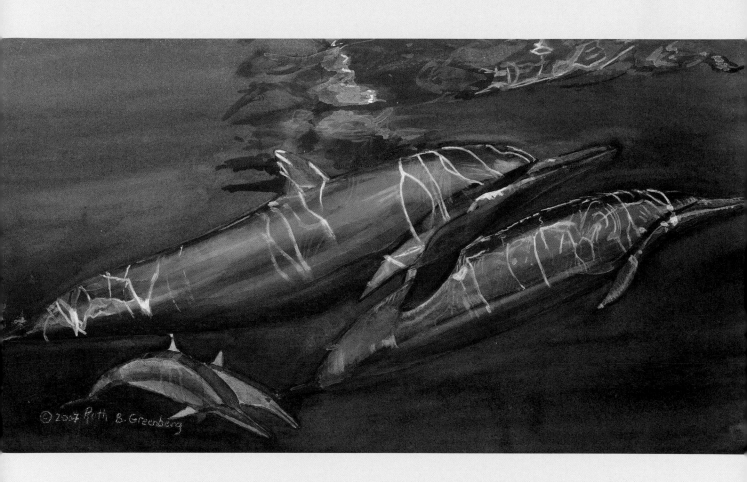

These cousins of Finn to him seem quite odd:
By hundreds they swim in a dolphin pod.

2

In his journey through the seas with his mother, Prudence, Finn had heard the sound of many other fin whales: some of them near, some of them far. Each whale had its own special sound, so he knew that wherever his mother might be, he would be able to **echo** her and, in a way that was almost telepathic, he would always be connected to her, though she might be an ocean away.

Just as Prudence was about to dive for a **bloom** of krill, she heard something that startled her, and she instinctively swam to Finn, though the alarming sound was several miles away from them in their feeding spot.

She caught his eye in an attempt to convey to him a sense of her urgency. She swam to Finn and nudged him, and then she began bounding up the length of the bay with as much haste as she could muster, away from the direction of the many distressed whale calls.

The speed at which the pair moved through the frigid sea agitated the waters of the bay, and all the sea life in their way. The seals scattered. The walruses jumped onto the icebergs in alarm. And even a polar bear quickly dog-paddled away from them.

Behind them, Prudence could hear a loud, constant humming sound. It was a ship with men. In the warmer waters, such ships were usually harmless as they rode over the waves, but the colder the climate, the more dangerous they became.

The ship was coming closer, and Prudence knew that she couldn't outrun it. No matter how fast a whale might swim, the ship was faster.

Finn meets the sea creatures, from wild to meek,
Like Pelican, with long and fish-filled beak.

She saw one of the men point a long weapon toward her off-spring. She swam to his side, hoping to draw the person's attention. She knew from experience that people would always take the easy target. But given the choice between a pair of easy targets, they would take the larger of the two.

She swam to Finn's side and bumped into him, just as he had done to her before their flight became desperate. At first he thought that the danger had passed, but then he felt her push him down, down into the depths of the bay, and he knew she was trying to protect him. They swam underwater for as long as they could, but he saw her losing her momentum and drift to the surface as the air in her lungs began to need replenishment. Just then, above the roar of the ship's engine, he heard an explosion. Then he saw it coming: the death-bringing barbed iron unfurling a coiled line, shooting toward Prudence.

When the harpoon hit, his mother writhed in pain as a storm-cloud of blood engulfed her. The coiled line dragged her above the waves as Finn watched helplessly. For a minute he watched, and then another. But still he waited, hoping that Prudence might somehow reappear, not wanting to believe what he knew to be true. And the minutes passed and passed, until they became nearly an hour.

And though she had not been gone an hour, it seemed as if she had gone a great while ago, such a distance there is between life and death.

Vanitas

3

Now he was all by himself, and the endless schools of cod and herring that swarmed indifferently around him only reminded him of his own separation from any other living thing in the cold, dark water.

He could hear plaintive sounds coming from back and forth across the bay. They were unlike any he had ever heard before.

One of the calls grew more and more distinct as it seemed to approach him, and he looked up warily in the direction of its coming.

It was a lone she-calf that swam toward him. She was lighter in color than Finn, with his dark grey upper body, and she had a less-prominent **dorsal fin**. She was a **blue whale**, the largest creature ever to live on the earth. She announced herself to Finn, though it took her some insistent repetition as her vocalization told him that her name was Cea.

She was a **baleen** whale just as he was, yet of a different **species**, and so their language was different.

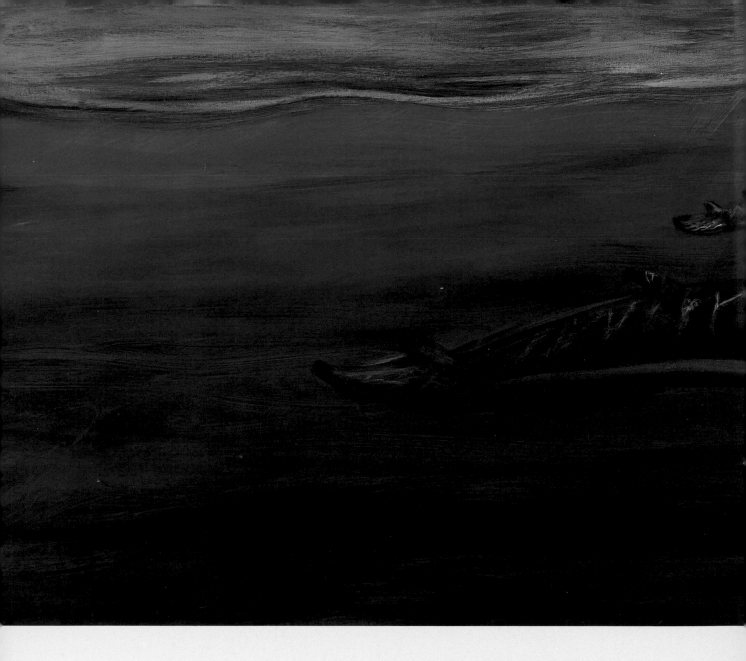

They worked with all their might to understand each other, and they produced similar noises of low pitch and high volume from deep within their larynxes, trying to make a commonality in their language. But her calls to him were of a different rhythm that made her echoes unintelligible, and he was no more successful in making himself comprehensible to her.

Searching for krill that will help him to grow,
Bull-calf and mother swim from floe to floe.

Despite the lack of communication between them, Finn could
understand that Cea had become newly orphaned that day and
in the same way that he had. His grief was lessened in some way
by the knowledge that he was not alone. Then they heard another.

They found a bull calf, younger and smaller than Finn, with no
mother nearby. Cea swam by the orphan and stroked it with her
flipper, aligning her eye to his, letting the creature know it was
no longer alone. She stayed there beside him.

Seven times, Cea repeated this mission, swimming to wherever she could detect the nearest anguished calls of an orphaned calf. Each time, a new member was added to the growing **pod**.

Finn looked about him. He was the only fin in a pod of eight blues. They were all smaller, which meant that the seven they had found were also younger. Finn had to infer all this for himself, though. The blue whales were all able to understand each other—but not him.

Though he felt a profound sense of separation from the rest of the pod, he also felt a profound need to help them.

This he knew: these calves were growing quickly and needed to find thousands of pounds of food each day that would keep them alive.

The krill dine where warm and cold currents meet:
To feed on them, Finn dives three hundred feet.

He could almost feel the spirit of his mother inside him, urging him to take over the care of the orphans, to lead them to food, to be the protector they now lacked.

He swam out in front of the pod, moving far enough in front of them that he could dive while facing them.

He looked expectantly at the other whales, hoping they would now follow his example and plunge down to where the upwelling currents brought the swarms of krill.

He swam beside Cea and caught her eye. Then he arched his back and dove. She followed him, and arriving at the spot in the ocean where the krill swirled underwater as if caught in a cyclone, Finn felt exaltation swirling through his own being as he watched her begin to feed alongside him.

When she had devoured a portion of the bloom, she ascended to the surface with Finn close behind. After a huge exhalation, Cea reached out and stroked the first orphan gently with her flippers and made a noise to him that Finn did not understand. Immediately, the orphan followed her down to the depths, where they stayed for several minutes before re-emerging.

She repeated this action with all the orphans in the pod, and Finn understood that now each calf had fed on the krill. He felt a bit left out of their communication and yet it was he who had enabled the orphans to survive that day.

Finn looked at his newly formed family.

His eye caught Cea's gaze while they logged, and he slapped the water once with his tail to make sure she knew that she was to follow him. For he was hearing a noise like rolling thunder, telling him something dreaded and deadly was now heading their way. And with that he dove as quickly and as steeply as his body would let him.

When orca breaches and falls on his side,
Mammals nearby should find places to hide.

Down into the water he started, and as he did, he heard her give a loud call that caught the attention of the other whales. Quickly she followed after him, and he went down as far as he could until he could descend no more. Then looking about him he was relieved to see her swimming there beside him. And then alongside her came another whale, and another, and another!

And then all seven of the orphans assembled beside Finn and Cea, down in the safety of the sheltering depths, and from three hundred feet above them came the sounds of a passing ship, its rumbling getting louder and louder and then fainter and fainter. Not until its dreadful noise was gone completely did they return to the surface.

Like bride and groom on a white wedding cake,
Cea and Finn love to ride a ship's wake.

4

Finn was getting better at communicating with Cea, and he could even make rudimentary communications with the other orphans.

It took some time before the rest of the orphaned pod felt a kinship with Finn.

As they headed off on their long sea-journey to the warm sunny waters, there was much that brought them together besides their common need for food. After a time, they began to understand that Finn was the leader. The blue whales were gratefully mystified by Finn's seemingly unerring ability to find their source of nourishment. What they didn't know of course was that Finn relied on the echoes from other fin whales who had found the abundance of krill in other parts of the ocean—fin whales could echo their finds for thousands of miles.

Finn and the orphans also took time at their feeding grounds to play and build up their strength. And here perhaps was where they bonded the most.

The whales in Finn's pod had favorite games, and among the most popular of all was **flipper-slapping**: it made a great crashing noise, and it sprayed great showers of water everywhere. Sometimes it annoyed the nearby whales from other pods and made them leave. And yet at other times, when the orphans wanted more company, it could also attract the attention of other whales. Either way, it was good.

If flipper-slapping was fun, then lob-tailing was even more fun. This was a great deal like flipper-slapping, but with a much larger surface of the **flukes** involved. This could be done while on one's belly or on one's back.

Going from tropical waters to chill,
whales swim a hemisphere searching for krill.

The most powerful variation on this game was the tail throw, or the **peduncle slap**. This involved more than just the flukes; it took the entire portion of one's lower body to perform, and with even more powerful results, of course.

When the whales were feeling less energetic, they were sometimes content merely to smack their jaws together or to slap their chins against the surface of the sea. No one could swim quietly on the surface for long, it seemed.

But there were times when everyone in the pod needed sleep. They handled their sleeping needs in various ways. It was perilous for whales to go completely asleep as they needed to breathe at regular intervals, even though they could slow this process and go without **breathing** for as long as thirty minutes.

But still they had to stay afloat as they slept, to be ever on guard against the perils of the sea, and so they slept with one half of their brains on and the other half off in a semi-conscious state. When in this mindset, they usually spent their time logging in stillness on the surface, but during times of **migration** they could even travel with half a brain asleep and the other half awake, reversing sides as needed, all the while swimming in formation while the lead whale stayed completely alert. This kind of drowsy travel could go on for hours each day.

The orphan pod spent many weeks in the warm waters of the ocean near the Equator—swimming, playing, feeding, and resting, day after day.

But the blooms of krill in the safety of the warmer waters now were dwindling and would not replenish for many months. If the pod remained, starvation in the equatorial waters was a certainty, so, reluctantly, they began their migration. To follow the krill upwellings meant to travel back northward, to the waters where they had all become orphans.

Having journeyed together from **pole** to Equator, Finn knew the way back with unerring accuracy. He and his fellow orphans could sense within their brains the earth's magnetic field. He knew that they were now heading back to **Arctic** waters.

Finn had a plan he believed would save them from the dangerous ships. He would not return to the same sea. Yes, he and the pod would travel further north, but they would find haven in one of the many other bodies of water, though still within Arctic waters.

Searching the ice, so hungry for mollusk,
Smiling, the walrus seems to be all tusk.

But then Finn sensed a larger pod of ships coming over the horizon, with many more ships than before.

By that time, Finn had stopped eating. The other whales of the pod were still filling their bellies with food. But Finn knew this was the time to flee. He began to slap his chin in the water.

The four youngest blue whales of the pod were Tera, Mystic, Salus, and Ceti, and they regarded Finn as an older brother: someone to look up to and to obey—most of the time.

As Finn began his chin slap, the four calves mirthfully slapped theirs as well. They continued until Finn swam away in great agitation.

Cea caught his eye. She tried to understand if there was something she needed to convey to the others, and if so, just what it was.

Finn began to wonder if his mind was playing tricks on him. Did he really remember the same ominous noise from so long ago, or had memory and fear distorted what he now thought he recalled?

Sensing him becoming less tense, Cea moved away, though not without some hesitation.

All around him were the whales he had come to love so much. The four little ones—Tera, Mystic, Salus, and Ceti—were still deep into their peduncle slapping game, which was nothing more than a silly excuse for making noise.

Nearby were Bale, Chord, and Laen, playing chase.

Finn knew now that he had not been wrong. The dreadful rumbling was back, and it was unmistakable.

And then some involuntary expression of pain and memory came roiling from within Finn: a long, mournful keening from deep within his chest, and it thundered across the water and filled the ear cavity inside the head of every member of the pod.

Cea was the first to understand what it meant. And she gave a cry that was different than Finn's and more intelligible to the rest of the pod.

All at once, they dove as they had done on the day they first came together as a pod.

Beneath the water they stayed, while the ships searched for prey. Finn called to the blue whales in a way that they could all understand. He turned away from the pod, his flukes to them, and he began swimming under the sea. They followed him and understood that he was leading them away from the ships, for they were his family.

It is no fluke, the great whales' distinction:
Do all you can to stop their extinction.

Glossary

Arctic: The area surrounding the North Pole.

baleen: The plates that hang down from a baleen whale's upper jaws. This is how baleen whales filter their food from the seawater. Baleen is made of keratin, just like your fingernails. Fin whales and blue whales have baleen. Some whales, such as sperm whales and killer whales, have teeth.

bloom: Krill congregate by the millions in what is called a swarm or a bloom. They do this for self-defense, because it is harder for a small predator to pick off an individual in a group. For a large predator like a whale, however, this makes them an ideal meal, as they can take krill into their mouths thousands at a time.

blubber: The layer of fat covering a whale's outer body keeps it warm and also acts as stored nourishment or energy.

blue whale: The largest of all whales. This baleen whale can grow to nearly 100 feet long (longer than an NBA court) and can weigh nearly 190 tons. Its tongue alone can weigh as much as an elephant. It is the largest animal known to have ever existed in the world.

breathing: When we humans breathe, our bodies can absorb around 15 percent of the oxygen inhaled. A whale, on the other hand, can absorb around 90 percent of the oxygen it inhales. Whales absorb this oxygen in myoglobin, a special protein found in muscles. Because of this, they can store oxygen more efficiently than we can. In addition, when whales dive, their hearts beat more slowly, and some of their arteries become constricted, slowing the flow of blood to organs without decreasing blood pressure. Whales can hold their breath for anywhere from 30 minutes to two hours, depending on the species. Most people can only hold their breath for around two minutes. David Blaine, who holds the world record, once held his breath for 17 minutes and 4 seconds.

calf: Cattle offspring are not the only young to be called calves; so are whale young. Even young camels, elephants, hippos, and rhinos are called calves.

Cetacea: Order of marine **mammals** known commonly as dolphins, porpoises, and whales. There are approximately 90 living cetacean species in the world today.

cormorant: Seabirds, found in coastal waters around the world, who happen to dive into the ocean in search of fish.

dolphin: There are many species of dolphins. They differ from baleen whales because they have teeth and do a bit more than echolocate. They have a 3-D sonar system built right in so they "see" three-dimensionally. This allows dolphins and other toothed **cetaceans** to use echolocation for hunting and navigation, while for baleen whales, echolocation is mainly used for communication.

dorsal fin: The fin on the back of a marine animal such as a whale or fish. It helps to stabilize the animal as it swims and turns.

A bard once did say, "All's well that ends well,"
As did our whale tale, and as did this shell.

echo: The repeated sound resulting from reflected sound waves.

echolocation: The biological sonar of animals, especially bats, dolphins, and whales.

eye contact: Whales can convey meaning to each other through eye contact, especially from mother to calf. Humans who have had eye contact with whales often claim that it is a life-changing experience.

fin or finback whale: The fastest of all whales, capable of speeds of up to 25 knots, or 25 nautical miles per hour. They can reach a length of 90 feet and a weight of up to 74 tons. They are considered an endangered species.

flipper-slapping: When a whale brings its flipper down against the surface of the water, creating a loud sound and splash.

flukes: The two lobes of a whale's tail are known as the flukes.

iceberg: Large floating masses of ice are found in the polar regions at either end of the earth, but the icebergs in Antarctica are far larger and more numerous than those in the Arctic.

krill: These small crustaceans are the primary food source of many whales, seals, penguins, and some fish. They are the largest protein source on earth.

logging: Whales lying at rest, often all in the same direction, are said to be logging because they look so much like logs floating on the water.

mammal: Any of the class of warm-blooded, fur-covered animals who feed their offspring with milk, including humans and whales, are mammals.

migration: Whales migrate or travel through all the oceans of the world to find food or bear offspring. The migration pattern of fin whales is relatively unknown.

peduncle slap: Also called the peduncle throw. The peduncle is the rear portion of the whale's torso, which the whale slaps or throws against the surface of the water, creating a loud noise and splash.

pod: Whales travel in groups known as pods. They do this for socialization and protection.

pole: The northernmost or southernmost point at each end of the earth is known as the pole.

species: A species is a category of scientific classification made up of organisms capable of interbreeding. There are 78 species of cetaceans, which include whales, porpoises, and dolphins.

spyhopping: When a whale raises itself vertically, with its upper half above the waterline to have a look around, they are both spying and hopping. If you can tread water while swimming, then like a whale, you too are spyhopping.

vanitas: A genre of art using symbols of mortality to show that all things of the world are but temporary.

whale: One of three air-breathing marine mammals included in the group known as cetaceans, which also includes porpoises and dolphins.

Humans will puzzle a whale to no end:
Will those who Finn meets be killer or friend?

Resources

Books

Abbey, Lloyd. *The Last Whales*. London: Transworld, 1989.

Ackerman, Diane. *The Moon by Whale Light and Other Adventures among Bats, Penguins, Crocodilians and Whales*. New York: Viking Books, 1992.

Burnett, D. Graham. *The Sounding of the Whale: Science and Cetaceans in the Twentieth Century*. Chicago: The University of Chicago Press, 2012.

Carwardine, Mark. Illustrated by Martin Camm. *Whales, Dolphins and Porpoises*. New York: Dorling Kindersley, 2002.

Chadwick, Douglas H. *The Grandest of Lives: Eye to Eye with Whales*. San Francisco: Sierra Club Books, 2006.

Cox, Lynne. *Grayson*. New York: Harvest, 2008.

Heller, Peter. *The Whale Warriors: The Battle at the Bottom of the World to Save the Planet's Largest Animals*. New York: Free Press, 2007.

Masson, Jeffrey Moussaieff, and Susan McCarthy. *When Elephants Weep: The Emotional Lives of Animals*. New York: Delta, 1995.

McClung, Robert M. Illustrated by William Downey. *Hunted Mammals of the Sea*. New York: William Morrow, 1978.

Nickerson, Roy. *Brother Whale*. San Francisco: Chronicle Books, 1977.

Nollman, Jim. *The Charged Border: Where Whales and Humans Meet*. New York: Henry Holt, 1999.

Payne, Roger. *Among Whales*. New York: Charles Scribner's Sons, 1995.

Peterson, Dale. *The Moral Lives of Animals*. New York: Bloomsbury Press, 2012.

Reeves, Randall R., et al. Illustrated by Pieter Folkens. *National Audubon Society Guide to Marine Mammals of the World*. New York: Chanticleer Press, 2002.

Siebert, Charles. Illustrated by Molly Baker. *The Secret World of Whales*. San Francisco: Chronicle Books, 2011.

Films

At the Edge of the World. Dir. Patrick Gambuti Jr. and Dan Stone. Endeavor Media. 2008. DVD.

Kingdom of the Blue Whales. National Geographic Television. 2009. DVD.

A Life among Whales. Dir. Bill Haney. Uncommon Productions. 2005. Netflix streaming.

National Geographic: Whales in Crisis. Dir. Bruce Norfleet. National Geographic Specials. 2004. DVD.

Nature: Fellowship of the Whales. Dir. Ross Isaacs. PBS Home Video. 2009. DVD.

Oceans. Dir. Jacques Cluzaud and Jacque Perrin. Narrator: Pierce Brosnan. Disneynature. 2009. DVD.

Secrets of the Deep (orig. title Ocean Odyssey). Dir. David Allen. BBC Worldwide. 2006. DVD.

The Whale Warrior: Pirate for the Sea. Dir. Ron Colby. Topics Entertainment. 2010. DVD.

Whale Wars: Season 1: Disc 1. Animal Planet. 2008. DVD.

Whaledreamers. Dir. Kim Kindersly. Monterey Media. 2006. DVD.

Whales: An Unforgettable Journey: IMAX. Dir. David Clark, Al Giddings, and Roger Payne. Slingshot DVD. 1998. DVD.

Online

Black, Richard. "Greenland Whale Hunt 'Commercial.'" bbc.co.uk. June 17, 2008.

Coronado, Rod. "Sinking the Icelandic Whaling Fleet." nocompromise.org. August 9, 2013.

"Evolution of Whale Animation." Smithsonian Museum of Natural History. August 9, 2013. Streaming video.

"Greenland Serving Whale Meat Dishes to Tourists." theguardian.com. June 26, 2013.

Horton, Jennifer. "How Eco-terrorism Works." howstuffworks. August 9, 2013.

"Inside Nature's Giants—The Fin Whale." BMETV.com. August 9, 2013. Streaming video.

"Japanese Whalers Accused of Dangerous Confrontation." thestandard.com.hk. August 9, 2013.

Keim, Brandon. "The Hidden Power of Whale Poop." Wired. August 9, 2012.

Kirby, David. "Japan Finally Comes Clean—They Don't Kill Whales for 'Science.'" TakePart. March 1, 2013.

Lyman, Rick. "How Iceland Whaling Was Crippled: It Was Easy." philly.com. November 14, 1986.

Poppick, Laura. "Icelandic Fin Whale Hunt Resumes, Stirs Debate." Yahoo News. June 23, 2013.

"Renegade Whaling: Iceland's Creation of an Endangered Species Trade." www.eia-international. org. July 2011.

Revkin, Andrew C. "Whale Hunters Hunted." NYTimes.com. January 12, 2008.

Ross-Flanagan, Nancy. "Whales of the Desert." Michigan Today. June 15, 2011.

Siebert, Charles. "The Social Lives of Whales." The Responsibility Project. August 9, 2013.

Thomas, Pete. "Dolphin 'Funeral' Videos Spark Discussions about Whether the Mammals Grieve." GrindTV. March 29, 2013.

———. "Dramatic Collision in Southern Ocean Leaves Anti-whaling Boat Damaged." GrindTV. March 8, 3013.

"The Truth about 'Scientific' Whaling." International Fund for Animal Welfare. August 9, 2013.

Winton, Richard. "Owner of Restaurant That Sold Whale Meat Faces Felony Counts." latimes. com. February 1, 2013.

The finback protects her baby from harm
And warns it of danger with eyes that alarm.

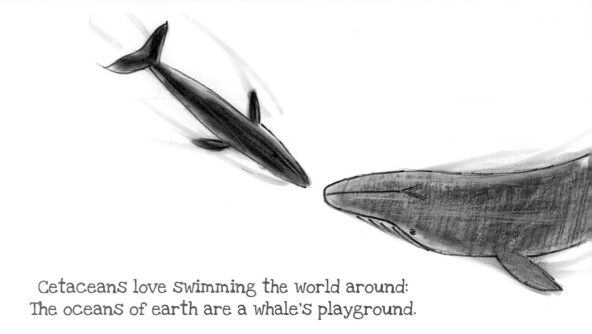

Cetaceans love swimming the world around:
The oceans of earth are a whale's playground.

A Note from the Illustrator

This book is a fictional account of an unfortunate journey of a heartfelt creature.

The International Whaling Commission (IWC) is an organization formed in 1946 to protect whales from being hunted to extinction, although no legal or financial consequences can be enforced to prevent whaling.

Fin whales are an endangered species, which means they are being hunted faster than they can repopulate. Iceland hunts the endangered fin whale and exports the meat to Japan for profit. Fin whales have spindle neurons, the brain cells that allow for emotion, memory, and decision making. Fin whales form bonds with each other, demonstrate altruism, and speak and navigate by sending sound waves out across the entire ocean.

Mother fin whales will save their calves by sacrificing themselves if a whale hunter approaches. The whales can even agree to meet at a certain time and place, and they strategize and adapt to avoid danger.

Fin whales are sentient creatures who communicate, feel, learn, and love.